The Lonely Rabbit

Arielle Wilson

AuthorHouse™
1663 Liberty Drive
Bloomington, IN 47403
www.authorhouse.com
Phone: 1 (800) 839-8640

© 2017 Arielle Wilson. All rights reserved.

No part of this book may be reproduced, stored in a retrieval system, or transmitted by any means without the written permission of the author.

Published by AuthorHouse: 07/13/2017

ISBN: 978-1-5246-9993-2 (sc)
ISBN: 978-1-5246-9994-9 (e)

Print information available on the last page.

Any people depicted in stock imagery provided by Thinkstock are models, and such images are being used for illustrative purposes only.
Certain stock imagery © Thinkstock.

This book is printed on acid-free paper.

Because of the dynamic nature of the Internet, any web addresses or links contained in this book may have changed since publication and may no longer be valid. The views expressed in this work are solely those of the author and do not necessarily reflect the views of the publisher, and the publisher hereby disclaims any responsibility for them.

authorHOUSE®

The Lonely Rabbit

Once, deep in the woods, there was a bunny named Peanut.

After a long winter, all the animals started to come out to play.

But, Peanut was all alone and had no one to play with.

Wanting to fit in, she tried to change herself to fit in with the cool cats of the woods.

And she didn't like to hunt.

But, one day the cats started picking on a mouse.

And Peanut knew it was wrong.

Even though she wanted to fit in with the cool cats, she knew it was wrong.

So she yelled "Stop! This is wrong."

The cats didn't like that so they started making fun of Peanut.

The called her names.

"You big baby! You can't even eat a little mouse!"

The cats said "You are not cool if you don't eat him."

Peanut knew it was wrong, and didn't want to be cool if it meant being mean.

So, she let the mouse go.

The cats got mad at Peanut...

and left her.

Peanut is proud that she did the right thing...

but is all alone again.

Then, far in the distance Peanut heard laughter and found a group of bunnies.

The rabbits saw peanut, and they let her play with them.

Peanut was no longer alone, and saw that the cats were never her friends. They wanted her to do something she knew was wrong. True friends wouldn't pressure others to do something that they didn't want to do.

CPSIA information can be obtained
at www.ICGtesting.com
Printed in the USA
BVOW05s2101180717
489653BV00008B/31/P

9 781524 699932